To Sophia,
May all your Christmas
wishes come true!

Love...................................

Sophia is ⇒**excited**⇐
Christmastime is here!

She says, "I wish for lots and lots of fluffy snow this year!"

Sophia writes to Santa.
The letter takes her ages.

"Perhaps I've wished for way too much..."
(There are over 50 pages!)

Dear Santa,

Sophia decorates the tree
with twinkly lights that glow.

Christmas
decorations

Look at Sophia up on stage.
She's in the Christmas play.

She wished to make her family proud and have the greatest day!

The kitchen's very busy.
Sophia can smell baking.

"I wish that I could eat that bowl of cake mix Dad is making."

Sophia wakes at 5 a.m.
"It's Christmas Day!
Yippee!"

She runs downstairs to find a pile of presents beneath the tree.

This jumper's really itchy.
She tries to grin and bear it.
Sophia really wishes that
she didn't have to wear it!

Sophia is so happy – her
wish for snow came true!

She's off to build a snowman now.
Perhaps she can build two!

Sophia is out sledging.
"I wish I could *speed* up!"

Her wish comes true,
her sledge is *fast*
when powered by a pup!

It's after Christmas dinner,
and everyone is snoring.
Sophia says to her best friend,
"I wish it was less **BORING!**"

Later, Mum asks Sophia,
"Did your **BIGGEST** wish come true?"
"Oh yes," she smiles,
"that wish was being…"

"...here with **all** of you!"

Do you wish for fun with friends,
or a family trip that never ends?
Whatever it is that you hold dear,
keep your Christmas wishes here!

I wish...

Written by J. D. Green
Illustrated by Julia Seal

www.hometownworld.co.uk

Follow us @hometownworldbooks

Put Me In The Story is a registered trademark of Sourcebooks, Inc.

ISBN 978-1-78553-995-4
All rights reserved
Printed in Italy
HTW_PO201806

Bestselling books starring your child!
www.putmeinthestory.co.uk

SANTA
STOP
HERE!